T0285629

VROOM TOWN VEHICLES

MARTA MAKES A MESS

Written by
Thomas Kingsley Troupe

Illustrated by
Brett Curzon

Table of Contents

A Shell Book

SEAHORSE PUBLISHING

Written by: Thomas Kingsley Troupe
Illustrated by: Brett Curzon
Design by: Under the Oaks Media
Series Development: James Earley
Editor: Erica Ellis

Library of Congress PCN Data
Marta Makes a Mess / Thomas Kingsley Troupe
Vroom Town Vehicles
ISBN 979-8-8904-2219-4 (hard cover)
ISBN 979-8-8904-2223-1 (paperback)
ISBN 979-8-8904-2227-9 (EPUB)
ISBN 979-8-8904-2231-6 (eBook)
ISBN 979-8-8904-2800-4 (read-along)
ISBN 979-8-8904-2804-2 (audio)
Library of Congress Control Number: 2023913209

Printed in the United States of America.

Seahorse Publishing Company

seahorsepub.com

Published in the United States
Seahorse Publishing
PO Box 771325
Coral Springs, FL 33077

CHAPTER 1

This is Marta.

Marta is a scooter.

Marta is a little scooter.

She lives in Vroom Town.

Marta likes her friends.

Marta and her friends play together.

They drive around Vroom Town Park.

"Let's drive through the sand," says Cody.

"We can splash through puddles," cries Hannah.

But Marta doesn't like to get dirty.

Marta likes to stay as clean as she can.

Marta watches her friends have fun.

Marta waits until they are done being messy.

"Come on, Marta," says Louie. "It's just a little dirt!"

Marta smiles and shakes her front tire.

"No, thank you," Marta says.

8

"It's raining," Hannah says. "Let's look for rainbows."

"I'll wait inside," Marta says.

"It's just a little water," says Hannah.

CHAPTER 2

Marta watches her friends play outside.

"Don't you miss having fun with them?" asks Dad.

"Yes," Marta says. "But I don't like being messy."

"Messes can be cleaned," says Dad. "Friends and fun are important."

Marta sees her friends the next day.

They are talking about the dirt bike race.

"I want to go!" says Louie.

"It will be fun to watch," Cody says.

"Dirt bikes are dirty," Marta says.
"Who wants that?"

"We do!" shout her friends.

Marta's friends all want to go and
watch the dirt bike race.

But she is not sure she will go.

CHAPTER 3

"Let's go, Marta!" Hannah says.

"I can't wait," Louie says.

Marta does not want to miss out.

Marta wants to be with her friends.

At the race, Marta watches the dirt bikes.

The bikes ride through the mud.

They jump into the air.

That looks like fun, thinks Marta.

Marta wants to try it too.

Marta drives over and joins the race.

Marta gets her tires in the mud.

"Marta is racing too?" Cody asks.

"She's going to get dirty!" cries
Hannah.

Marta races with the dirt bikes.

She laughs and gets mud everywhere.

Marta is making a mess!

After the race, Marta drives to her friends.

Marta is covered in mud.

"Wow, Marta!" Louie cries. "You're muddy!"

"But I had fun," Marta says. "That's what matters!"

Marta now knows that trying new things is fun. And sometimes fun is messy!